First edition for the United States
published 1988 by Barron's
Educational Series, Inc.

Copyright © in this edition Century Hutchinson Ltd 1988

First published 1988 by
Hutchinson Children's Books
An imprint of Century Hutchinson Ltd
London, England

Designed by ACE Limited

All inquiries should be addressed to:
Barron's Educational Series, Inc.
250 Wireless Boulevard
Hauppauge, New York 11788

Library of Congress Catalog Card No. 87-24175

International Standard Book No. 0-8120-5901-8

Library of Congress Cataloging-in-Publication Data
Poole, Josephine.
    Puss in boots
    illustrated by Edmund Morin; adapted by Josephine Poole.
    Adaptation of the traditional fairy tale Chat botté by Charles Perrault.
    Summary: A cunning cat wins for his master a castle and the hand of a princess.
    [1. Fairy tales. 2. Folklore – France]   I. Poole, Josephine.   II. Perrault, Charles,
    1628-1703. Chat botté.   III. Title.
    PZ8.M826Pu 1988 [E]   87-24175
    ISBN 0-8120-5901-8

Printed in Italy by New Interlitho s.p.a.

890 987654321

PUSS IN BOOTS

ILLUSTRATED BY
EDMUND MORIN

ADAPTED BY JOSEPHINE POOLE

BARRON'S

NEW YORK

There was once a miller who earned much and spent much, so that when he died he left nothing but his mill, his donkey, and his cat. He had three sons. The eldest moved into the mill, and the second took the donkey so the youngest son got only the cat.

He sat down in a field and groaned aloud. "What will become of me?" he cried. "It's all very well for my brothers! If they work together they are set up for life, but what can I do with a cat? I am afraid I shall starve to death." And the poor fellow's eyes filled with tears.

Then up spoke the cat, and the strange thing was that the young man could understand every word he said. "My dear master, things are not always as bad as they appear. If you will make me a pair of boots, so that I can scamper through dirt and brambles without hurting my soft paws, you may find that you have the best of the bargain."

The young man was touched by this speech and felt suddenly hopeful, for in the past he had often admired the cleverness of this cat. So he obtained a pair of little leather boots, as well as a strong drawstring bag that the animal asked for.

Mr. Puss pulled on the boots, which fitted him perfectly. Then he put some lettuce into the bag and crept away into the thickest part of the hedge. Here he arranged his bag so that the top was wide open. Stretching himself out beside the bag, he lay quite still, as if he were dead. But all the time he held on to the strings of the bag with his front paws.

It was not long before a silly rabbit hopped up and fearfully examined the cat – but he did not move a whisker. Next the rabbit began poking about the bag to see what it contained. It smelled nice. Before long he ventured in. Puss promptly drew the strings, and the rabbit was a prisoner. He heaved him up on his shoulder, and set off at once for the King's palace.

It was a very hot day, and the way was long and dusty. But the cat trudged on, until at last he arrived at the gate. He told the guard that he wanted to speak to the King, and he was shown upstairs to His Majesty's apartment.

He laid down the rabbit in front of the King and made a low bow. "Sire," said he, "I come from my lord the Marquis of Carabas." This was the title he had invented for his master. "He desires me to present you with this rabbit from his warrens, with his greetings and best wishes."

The King was somewhat astonished, but he answered politely with his thanks to the Marquis. And the cat went away.

The next time he went out very early and hid with his bag in a cornfield until he caught some partridges. These too he presented at the palace, and the King was pleased. After this he often received game from the Marquis.

One day the King went out driving with his daughter, the most beautiful princess in the world. The cat ran at once to his master and said, "Go to the river, take off your clothes, and jump in! Ask no questions, but do what I say, and your fortune is made." Then he scampered away and took his master's clothes and hid them under a stone. Before long he saw the royal carriage and began to shout, "Help! Help for the Marquis of Carabas! Robbers have stolen his clothes and left him to drown."

The King ordered his guards to rescue the young man. He took him into his carriage and lent him a suit from the royal baggage. Then the boy looked so handsome that the Princess immediately fell in love with him. The three drove on together.

Meanwhile, the cat ran ahead and found some reapers out in the fields. "When the King passes you must pretend that all this belongs to the Marquis of Carabas," he ordered. "Otherwise, I will make mincemeat of you!" The were so frightened that they obeyed him.

At last the cat came to a great castle, which belonged to a wicked ogre. He was exceedingly rich and owned all the fields of hay and corn along the road. He also possessed a magic power: he could turn himself into any shape he wanted.

But Mr. Puss had found out all about the ogre and his magic power. He darted into the castle and leaped up the stairs to the very top. There he found the ogre sitting alone in a little room, drinking beer. They exchanged greetings, and the ogre was as polite as it was possible for him to be. He looked at the cat now and then with greedy eyes, however, as though he might like to make a meal of him.

"I have heard many tales of the marvelous shapes you can change yourself into," began the cat, trying not to shiver. "They say you can become a lion, or an elephant, or a bear, whenever you like, but really I can't believe it."

The ogre roared and, dashing his mug of beer upon the ground, instantly changed into a lion. Poor Pussy was so alarmed that he fled out of the window and scrambled to safety as fast as he could.

Then the ogre resumed his natural shape, and the cat came down, still trembling.

"That gave you a fright!" rumbled the ogre, with a cruel grin. And he slapped his great thigh.

"So it did," said the cat, trying to keep his voice steady. "I admit you have partly convinced me –"

"What do you mean?" bellowed the ogre, his small eyes burning red with rage.

"You are big and fierce, and you turned yourself into something that is also big and fierce. Perhaps that isn't so difficult to do! I think it might be very much harder for you to change into something little and helpless – a mouse, for instance."

No sooner said than done. The ogre vanished with a roar that dwindled into a squeak, and a tiny gray mouse scuttled across the floor. Puss pounced – and gobbled him up!

The next moment he heard carriage wheels running over the drawbridge.

The King had noticed the ogre's fine castle as he was driving past and decided to pay him a visit. The cat was just in time to greet him in the courtyard. "Welcome to the home of my lord the Marquis of Carabas," he said, with a deep bow.

The King looked around, impressed with the splendor of everything. The cat led the way into the banquet hall, where a feast was waiting for the ogre's friends. Seeing that the King was there, however, they did not dare to enter. The King sat at the head of the table. His daughter and the miller's son sat on his right and left, and Puss stood upon a stool. The ogre's servants passed the dishes and poured the wine. The Princess and the young man looked lovingly at each other as they ate. And the King was truly delighted with the refined manners and handsome figure of his host the Marquis.

"You have rich estates, my Lord, and a splendid castle," he said at last, "I'll speak plainly! I can see that my daughter is head over heels in love. And for my part, I'll be glad to have you as my son-in-law."

So the blushing young man took the most beautiful of princesses for his bride. The wedding was celebrated that same afternoon.

As for the cat, he was made a Lord, and he never chased mice any more – except for his own amusement.